D1015531

Dear Parents, Educators, and Guardians,

Thank you for helping your child dive into this book with us. We believe in the power of books to transport readers to other worlds, expand their horizons, and help them discover cultures and experiences that may differ from their own.

We also believe that books should inspire young readers to imagine a diverse world that includes them, a world in which they can see themselves as the heroes of their own stories.

These are our hopes for *all* our readers. So come on. Dive into reading and explore the world with us!

Best wishes,
Your friends at Lee & Low

Hooks, Gwendolyn,author.
Buddy bench

2019
33305246701027
ca 09/24/19

READING!

The Buddy Bench

by Gwendolyn Hooks

illustrated by Shirley Ng-Benitez

Lee & Low Books Inc. New York

Dedicated to those with friends and those in need of a friend.
Reach out and have fun together. —G.H.

To the reader: find an undiscovered buddy in your class
or at recess and greet 'em with a smile. —S.N-B.

Text copyright © 2019 by Lee & Low Books Inc.
Illustrations copyright © 2019 by Shirley Ng-Benitez
All rights reserved. No part of this book may be reproduced, transmitted, or stored
in an information retrieval system in any form or by any means, electronic, mechanical,
photocopying, recording, or otherwise, without written permission from the publisher.
LEE & LOW BOOKS Inc., 95 Madison Avenue, New York, NY 10016, leeandlow.com
Book design by Maria Mercado
Book production by The Kids at Our House
The illustrations are rendered in watercolor and altered digitally
Manufactured in China by Imago
Printed on paper from responsible sources
(hc) 10 9 8 7 6 5 4 3 2 1
(pb) 10 9 8 7 6 5 4 3 2 1
First Edition

Library of Congress Cataloging-in-Publication Data
Names: Hooks, Gwendolyn, author. | Ng-Benitez, Shirley, illustrator.
Title: The buddy bench / by Gwendolyn Hooks; illustrated by Shirley Ng-Benitez.
Description: First edition. | New York: Lee & Low Books Inc., [2019] |
Series: [Dive into reading ; 7] | Summary: When Padma notices a boy
sitting by himself every day, she enlists her friends to create a buddy
bench, where anyone at school can go if they want or need a friend.
Identifiers: LCCN 2018049338 | ISBN 9781620145715 (Hardcover)
ISBN 9781620145722 (Paperback)
Subjects: | CYAC: Benches—Fiction. | Schools—Fiction. | Friendship—Fiction.
Classification: LCC PZ7.H76635 Bud 2019 | DDC [E]—dc23
LC record available at https://lccn.loc.gov/2018049338

Contents

Old Friends 4

Buddy Bench 14

New Friends 24

Old Friends

It was the first day of school.
Padma was ready early.
She waited outside for her friends.

"Have you been out here all night?"
asked Henry.
"No," said Padma.
"But I can't wait for school to start."

"Here come Mei, Lily, and Pablo," said Henry.

"Finally!" said Padma.
"Let's go!"

At school they looked
for their classroom.
"Oh no!" said Lily.
"We are all in the same class.
But not Padma."

"I'm next door," said Padma.
"You will be all alone," said Lily.
"It's okay," said Padma.
"I like to make new friends."

At lunch Padma sat with
her old friends.
"I see some of the kids
in my class," said Padma.

She waved them over to the table.
"I'm Pablo," said Pablo.
"Hi," said Padma's new friends.

At recess everyone played games.
Padma played with her old friends.
Padma played with her new friends.

They all jumped rope together.
It was a great first day of school.

Buddy Bench

One day Padma saw a new boy standing alone by the fence. "I wonder why he's all alone," she said to Lily.

"It's not easy for everyone to make new friends," said Lily. The boy left before they could say hi.

"I have an idea,"
said Padma.
"Let's make a place
where kids can go
if they feel lonely."

"What kind of place?" asked Mei.
"We can make a Buddy Bench!"
said Padma.

"Let's paint the bench," said Henry.
"Let's paint it yellow and purple," said Lily.
"Let's make a sign. Then everyone will know where to go to meet new friends," said Padma.

"We need to ask Principal Hart," said Pablo.

They went to the principal's office. Principal Hart said the Buddy Bench was a great idea.

On Saturday, they painted the bench. They made a Buddy Bench sign.

Then Padma made up a song about the bench.

They sang the words as they jumped rope.

After a few days everyone
was singing the song.
But no one sat
on the Buddy Bench.

New Friends

Weeks passed and still no one sat on the Buddy Bench. Then one day Padma saw the new boy sitting on the Buddy Bench.

"Let's go!" said Padma
to her friends.

"Hi! I'm Padma," said Padma.
"What's your name?"
"Zander," said the boy.

"Hi," said Mei. "Did you just move here?"

"Yes. My mom is an army pilot," said Zander.
"We move around a lot."

"Moving is not always fun,"
said Lily.
"It's hard to make new friends."

"We would like to be
your friends," said Padma.
"Do you want to play?"
asked Zander.
"I like slides."
"Me too!" said Padma.

Padma played with her
old friends.
Padma played with her
new friends.
They all played together.

Activity

Have more fun with this book!

1. Was there a time when you helped someone who was lonely? Have you ever felt lonely? What did you do?

2. Does your school or a nearby park have a Buddy Bench? Do you think the Buddy Bench is a good idea? Why or why not?

3. With help from an adult, write a letter to the principal of your school about how a Buddy Bench could help students.

4. Think of another idea besides a Buddy Bench to help a new student make friends.

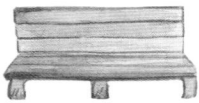

Gwendolyn Hooks has written several children's books, including Bebop Books's *Can I Have a Pet?* and Lee & Low's *Tiny Stitches*. When she was a child, her family moved often, and her first stop in every new city was the library. Gwen lives in Oklahoma City, Oklahoma, with her family.

Shirley Ng-Benitez loves to draw and write. She creates her art with watercolor, gouache, pencil, and digital techniques. She lives in the San Francisco Bay Area, and is inspired by nature, her family, her pup, and her two kittens.

Read More About Padma and Her Friends!